This and That and an Ice Cream Sundae

Reflections in Poems from Age 86

Dr. Marlou Newkirk

Nuhawk, LLC

For permissions for reprinting visit:
MarlouNewkirk.com

ISBN #978-1-7379340-1-1

Editor Laurie Newkirk
Cover and Book Design by Vincent Legg

Photographers / Artists:
Stick Figure / Matthias Enter plus Daniel Berkmann / Adobe Stock, Vintage Mirror/BrAt82 / Adobe Stock, Ice Cream Sundae / BillionPhotos.com / Adobe Stock, Storm Cloud and Rainbow on Beach / Olha Rohulya / Adobe Stock, Seagull on Beach / Deana / Adobe Stock, Birch Leaves in Forest / Lakov Kalinin / Adobe Stock, Winter Snow / Alexander Ozerov / Adobe Stock, Yellow Daffodils / Lumikk555 / Adobe Stock, Grand Central Station / Vincent Legg, New York Street / Rawf8 / Adobe Stock, Ready for Yard Sale / Africa Studio / Adobe Stock, Tea Cup with Tea Leaf / DN6 / Adobe Stock, Ready to Play / Soupstock / Adobe Stock, Vintage Pen and Paper / Nattapol Sritongcom / Adobe Stock, Mountain Road / Hale M. Kell / Adobe Stock, Marlou Newkirk Headshot / Vincent Legg

Published by Nuhawk, LLC
117 Putnam Ave, Suite 248
Riverside, CT
NuhawkLLC.com

About the Author

At age 77, Dr. Marlou Newkirk took a class and fell in love with writing. She then joined a writers' group and then another and another. At 82, she finally fulfilled her dream: she became a published writer. Since then, she has gone on to become an award-winning author of both short stories and magazine articles. Now, at 86, she is proud to be releasing her first book of poetry.

Before becoming a writer, Marlou earned a doctorate in Education from Columbia University and spent many years at the forefront of adult education in New York City.

This book is dedicated to:

My daughter, Laurie Newkirk, and my son-in-law,
Vincent Legg, who bring me joy and happiness, whom
I love so very much, and without whom this book would
never have been created.

My sister, Kelly Barrett, for her love, kindness and
wisdom and who has always been there for me, no matter
what. My brother-in-law, Brooks Barrett, for his
generosity and love of family.

My brother, Bill Jahn, sister-in-law, Karen Jahn,
niece, Lindsay Kessler, for their love, courage, stability,
sense of adventure and devotion to family.

CONTENTS

Opening Poem

About Me

Nature

New York City

Potpourri

Final Thought

ACKNOWLEDGMENTS

To my families, I love you all: Barretts, Cianos, DeMarinos, Fishers, Haumanns, Jahns, Kesslers, Leggs, Milmoes, O'Briens

Laurie Newkirk for her creative vision and planning
Vincent Legg for his fabulous book and cover design
Barbara Wilkov for her eagle-eye proofreading
Steve Morenberg for his insightful comments
Caroline Suozzi for her assistance with my website

Bigelow Senior Center Poetry Group:
Emerson Gilmore, brilliant poet, wise, gentle leader;
Richard Anderson, Edward Ahern, Patricia Clark,
Gerard Coulombe, Mary Grace Dembeck, Dru Martin

Fairfield Library Saturday Writing Group:
Alex McNab, founder, brilliant writer, knowledgeable, inspiring leader; Richard Anderson, Silvia Hines, Emerson Gilmore, Martin Kivell, Janet Rosenblum

Edward Ahern, Alison McBain, dazzling poets, prolific innovative genre writers, founders Poets' Salon
Gabi Coatsworth, superb writer, gifted communicator, founder Writers' Rendezvous, invaluable newsletter
Carol Danhauser, wonderful writer, inventive, founded Fairfield County Writers' Studio, peaceful writers' space

Geoffrey Morris, Robin Phillips, Megan Smith-Harris and the TownVibe team for their tremendous talent and helping to launch my professional writing career

Clara Moisello, Antonio Espinoza, leaders non-violent
communication groups where I learn so much

My original meditation group: Alice Mindrum,
founder, learned, kind: Frances Baldwin,
Barbara Capasso, John Desrochers, Cornelia Fortier,
Mary Ellen Hagedus, Sarah Johnson,
Donnatella Nichols, Mazie Ohm, Paul Whitman,
Hilary Williams, Rosemary Williams

Friends: Frances Baldwin, Stephanie Carrow,
Fontaine Dunn, Lionel Ketchian, Maria Lannon,
Patty Loh, Janet Luongo, Rita Lund, Marie Martinez,
Jacque Masumian, Kathryn Mayer, Nirmala Momaya,
Khorshed Randeria, Victoria Sherrow, Betty Salzer,
Bill Voegele, Donna Ward

Dr. Carol Hendricks whose wonderful advice
and insights have helped me to 86
Dr. Veronica Waks, my friend and doctor who,
also, helped me to 86
Kim Ciano always supportive and a front line
nurse during the pandemic
Melissa Arnold and Jonathan Davis, masters of
exercise who keep me moving

My core doctors for the amazing care I have received
Drs: Peter Bongiorno, Janice Hunt, David Lomnitz
James Samuel, Marc Weizman, wonderful support staffs

James Legg Jr., Mary DeMarino, Ann DeMarino,
John DeMarino Sr., Cindy DeMarino, Joyce Feidler,
who are always with us in spirit

Why I Write

I write because my brain drips ideas
into my fingers which fly across a keyboard
Can't sleep, write poems, stories in my head

Orange, cotton candy sunsets
How do I describe these to others
Express feelings of euphoria
Relate sheer raw beauty of them

Writing gives my life meaning
To tell a story, examine, explore
Try to make sense out of
disturbing events
Sharing is a tremendous gift

I belong to a community who gives
empathy, inspiration,
kindness, are non-judgmental
Am in awe of their abilities

What would I have during this pandemic
without writing groups
I create to use my mind, help my soul,
stave off anxiety attacks, depression
I am blessed, so blessed.

About Me

My Name is Marlou

I lay as a newborn in my mother's arms
She whispered into my tiny shell-like ear
There are three things
that will determine your life
If I had had the strength in my tiny fist
I would have reached up and punched her

First, I will name you Marlou
after your Scot granny Martha and
your German granny Louisa
An attempt at reconciliation
as she did not get along with either
A futile effort as we rarely saw them
Have had to spell my name every day of my life

Second, you will become an actress and
fulfill my fantasy of being one. Cruel

Third, I will make you into my image
you will; Look like me, Talk like me,
Think like me. Doubly cruel

She loved me. I know that
But the demands were great
Have compassion now
but not then

My Father came to us clinically depressed
He struggled valiantly to support us
He would erupt. Terrifying

They lay together in a cemetery
under one tombstone
In peace as they never were in life
They whisper into the wind and I hear it
We are waiting for you
We are waiting for you

When I Look in the Mirror

When I look in the mirror I see a face tired
worn but not old
a word I do not use for anyone

I prefer antique

Perhaps I should go on Antique Road Show and
get an appraisal?

Is being born in one era vs another better?
Louis XIV chair more valuable than a Louis XVI?

Can they feel the emotions lived, survived:
love, joy, ecstasy
sorrow, grief, bitterness?

Do I get credit for:

the many times I have stumbled, fallen, gotten up and
kept on walking

things I have tried to fight against:
prejudice, misogyny, injustice
a journey stopped only by death

Could you give me an approximation of my worth?

Lists Wherefore

List, lists, so many lists I don't adore

Wash the dishes, scrub the floor,

clean out closet, rearrange the drawer

Self-improvement long list to be sure

Items to be delivered from online store

Write in notebooks, rarely used, but buy more

Can't find last one, swore and swore

List on paper must have flown out the door,

happily gone forevermore

Other people check done, satisfaction galore

But lists overwhelm and make my head sore

It's clear to see lists I absolutely abhor

I dislike them to my very core.

Boldness Has Genius

Everything in my home must go
A bold statement
but can no longer live with clutter

Clutter keeps you chained to the past
mortgages your future
does not allow you to live in the present

Researchers have declared
people hate to lose things
more than they like to win

I go through boxes
deal with sadness
remembrance of things past

Papers, books I have saved
are items I was going to read Someday
Someday eludes me

The more I throw out
the more I can
Am falling in love with magic of open spaces

A Memory: Ice Cream Sundaes

When I was a child, nine or ten, my mother, sister and I
would go to a restaurant, Stouffers, where we would
crawl up on stools and order ice cream sundaes.

Sundaes: vanilla ice cream, hot molten chocolate, dab of real
whipped cream, cherry on top and pecans,
starting for me a lifelong love of this exotic nut.

Had my mother known of the benefits of dark chocolate,
had the money held, we surely would have ordered seconds
notwithstanding the sugar shock sure to occur.

This feast preceded by a movie, perhaps a fun
"Road" one starring Bob Hope and Dorothy Lamour
or Judy Garland in "Meet Me in St. Louis."

These peaceful outings were a godsend to us
as ours was a tumultuous household.
When I was eight anxiety came to live with us.
Attached to everyone like a parasite finding a host.

It stayed with us all our lives. When it hits me now,
I do what the experts suggest; I try to think of a happy place
Stouffers, three stools, and ice cream sundaes.

Six Fathoms Deep

If only the sea would calm down
I am the sea and the sea is me
Turbulent and then calm
We have mood swings

Mine are generated because
Divers can see the flora and fauna
But no one can see my creative center
The beauty that lies within

Machines are made that access
Every part of my body
But not my soul
Where is my glass bottom boat

My Soul

Lost my soul. Went looking for her
on beach in Southport.
Where have you been she cried?
Sorry. Worked in such soulless
place didn't realize you were missing.
Promise never to be absent again.

Turned our attention to beauty
around us. Day after storm,
another rising. Horizon pitch black,
water churning. Seashells embedded
in damp brown sand only bright color
in this dark, wild landscape.

Beach littered with broken bamboo-like
reeds. No birds, mallard ducks, one lone
seagull standing at water's edge.
Ice-age grey boulders lay against wall.
Sky ominous. We should leave.

Speak Kindly

In the human body
there are 206 bones
and approximately
650 muscles
360 joints
900 ligaments
4000 tendons

One of these parts cries out for attention every day
If it does not get it, punishes with aches, pains
They need lotions, potions, ointments
Want to try marijuana

We speak harshly of the body
Twisted ankle, wrenched knee,
back spasms, joint aches

Perhaps if spoken kindly to:
thanked for every act done:
carrying up steep stairs,
shoveling deep snow,
driving dangerous highways,
walking anywhere,
it would not punish so much

Decay

Never thought about body's decay

Knew systems fail near death

kidneys stop, heart ceases

Still in life, teeth break, bones creak

Myofascial new in vocabulary

means muscles can hurt like hell

Itises: tendinitis, bursitis, arthritis

not friends

Gather ye rosebuds fine but have

to have parts that work to do so

Had known there was a shelf life

enjoyed previous, precious years

more before rot set in

Will continue to patch, patch, patch

go into world like a bandaged scarecrow

Asparagus, No Thanks

I was ten when I went to sleep-away camp
Loved it – away from my dysfunctional family
Learned archery, tennis, played soccer, swam
were crafty crafts, lots of singing at bonfires

One incident stands out for me
Sadistic 17-year-old camp counselor
made me sit at dinner table 'til I had eaten
pale green, slimy, right out of a can asparagus

Had no coping skills for I was ten
Doris Day's record "Sentimental Journey"
on sound system. Was on own journey
trying not to gag by forcing slimy mess
down my throat

Now, restaurants think it posh to offer
fresh luminous green asparagus. I opt
for green beans and wonder how the
counselor's prison guard career worked out

Circus No

Went to circus as child
Anticipation, excitement, tent,
Crowds, cotton candy, popcorn
But my childhood anxiety
saw danger everywhere

The Flying Wallendas might
miss bar one day, netless
fall to horrible death

Lion might decide to hell
with whip lashing out at him
rip the trainer's face off

The scantily clad women
high atop elephants might have
forced themselves not to look
down, death staring them in face

Riding horse bareback is hard
Four riders standing bareback, insanity
Again, don't look down
hooves, waiting to crush to death

Never found the clowns funny
Found scary
Some grown men in clown outfits
do terrible things to women

You can see no circus is
ever going to hire me
to do publicity for them

Nature

—✳—☀—✳—

Beauty Unfolds

Letting go of winter isn't a big loss
to those who don't revel in
stark branches, dirty snow mounds, short dark days
barely sunshine, cars encased in snow, black ice,
shoveling, dry skin, cold hands, depression
It's not only fog that comes slowly, quietly
but spring – eager do we wait
Slowly, the dew drops, crocus appear
low to the ground not to be blown over by March winds
Forsythia's tiny yellow flowers emerge
gingerly over the bush as though taking test run
to see if frost will appear
Braver daffodils tout hardy green leaves,
unfold quickly
Their cousins, tulips, make their appearance
all colors even blue/black
Spring is sensual
Sweet-smelling hyacinths
Pink azalea bushes
Lilacs dazzle eyes
Lovely to smooth hand over pussy willows
Sounds of birdsong
thrilled to hear these old friends
Do not want to rush spring, want to enjoy
process of unfolding

Chestnut Tree

Tree

lives on

other side of

my terrace, chestnut

nuts big as tennis balls

hard as rocks, squirrels ignore

too big to carry, impossible to eat

Squirrels run up and down tree, chase

each other having fun it seems to onlooker

Tree last to generate leaves, first to drop in fall

Each spring worry that tree is dead, stark and naked but

gradually leaves unfold delighting me, fun loving squirrels

Winter Haikus

Winter has beauty
snowy white fields, ice sculptures
Could forgo it all

Winter could be fun
Skate, ski, sled, make snow persons
Prefer to live Spain

Yes, I hate winter
Not supposed to hate nature
Forgive me I do

Best of Time, Worst of Time

Spring, surely best time of year
From damp, dangerous winter
into the slowly recovering earth
Everything growing brighter
sun colored daffodils, forsythia
As sun grows stronger
perky red tulips, sweet fragrant lilacs
Trees delicately dressed at first
then in full attire, green of all shades

For some spring is the worst
pollen in air—allergies
Not able to breathe scented air
nor focus on blue skies, drifting clouds
Grumble about the rains
For them spring is full of misery

Oh, would that I could live
in a paradise where spring is eternal

New York City

Vacation and Vacuum Cleaner

Need vacation and need vacuum cleaner

Floors are dusty, dust balls abound

Need vacation, soul is dusty

Can't afford both right now

Few have died from dusty floors

But people have just lain down and died from dusty souls

Need to shake free. Need to experience another place

Take day trip. Train to New York City

Train whizzes past greenery, towns

Energized by people in Grand Central

Get out of my way busy

Walk up Fifth Avenue to a cacophony of horn sounds.

Honk in code: MOVE

Arrive at Rockefeller Center—still there

Trot on up to the Metropolitan Museum of Art
—still there

Feel soul dust dissolving

Reverse trip—whizzing past greenery and towns

Soul cleaner now

Will take care of floor dust in time—there is time

Typical Day New York City

Walking up Fifth Ave
enjoying the warm weather
see crowd ahead on 38th Street
Bus stopped, door open, driver
standing middle of the avenue
screaming at motorist,
motorist screaming back
Assumed he had cut bus driver off

Meanwhile, traffic backed far up the avenue
Bus driver went back to bus, got on steps,
mad still, got off steps, went back to scream
No blows going to be exchanged
crowd got bored, moved on
Forgotten by 39th Street

Abandoned

They lie discarded, dead-like, against buildings

Humans withered by anguish

Are passersby horrified, compassionate?

Children once. Families helpless—grieve

Scooped up, hosed down, put in dangerous shelters

Do not want them to freeze. How would that look?

I see and say, thereby for the grace of heaven go I

Bus Ride Uptown

New York City on a Thursday evening
I left the movie theatre
about 9pm, waited at 72nd Street
boarded an uptown Broadway bus
destination 120th Street—home

Bus not crowed, plenty of seats
At 86th Street large man got on dripping blood
down from his left knee
large slit in pants oozed blood
Bus driver stared straight ahead
as man dropped coins into ticket box

Limped to seat facing the aisle
I, far back, was not threatened by blood
He was very quiet, did not move
Probably lost a lot of blood
he was still dripping

My first reaction was did he not
have someone to take him to hospital
I knew that's where he was going
Never knew anyone who had to go alone
did he not have money for cab
On reflection, cab would not have taken him

Then began to wonder what happened
Thought perhaps a bar fight but in any
movies I had seen, guns used
Perhaps on upper west side of Manhattan
knife was weapon of choice

At 114th Street he exited
limped to St. Luke's Hospital
How did this saga end
Was other person involved waiting at ER
Were police called

Just another story in the thousands of stories
that happen on a Thursday night
at about 9pm in New York City

Potpourri

H*A*I*R

You really can take it anywhere
Careful one doesn't get a spare
Morning looks like grizzly bear
or wandered into lion's lair
or tangled mane on mare
Thousand creative ways to wear
Tease, tease high into the air
Dye Easter egg colors—flair
Odd style does get you stare
Cut too short at stylist swear
Bad hair day leads to despair
Expensive products to repair
Twist, twirl curling iron beware
singed ends worst nightmare
in frustration out will tear
Know love/hate is this affair

Ode to Westport Drivers How I Hate Thee

Where in hell are you going that you have to
drive so fast
        Reckless   Reckless   Reckless

Traffic lights: Red, Yellow, Green all mean
        GO   GO   GO

Weather ignored. Sun, snow drive the same
Skid, slip, slide
        Feckless   Feckless   Feckless

Honk! They want me to fly over car in front of me
Pass me, rude gesture. Young heads in car
        Bad Role Model: Bad Bad Bad

In desperation I take to back roads
Attitude there:
Maybe we will share the road, maybe we won't
Don't stop at stop signs
        Shame   Shame   Shame

On foot most Westporters are nice people
Driving they are
        Maniacs   Maniacs   Maniacs

Come to Tea

I have a friend Bruce Moose
He thinks he is a goose
Silly, silly Bruce Moose
Can't fly, falls on caboose
I have a friend an elephant
Ellie reads, writes, is intelligent
On problematic politicians eloquent
Her knowledge and ideas relevant
My friend sad Brian Bumblebee
Visits, we talk, give him Brie
No longer sad is he
Even feels a little glee
If you want to visit with me
You must definitely stay for tea
We will have a party
My three friends and thee

Johnny

Johnny is playing high school football

His meanspirited, loudmouthed father

screams at every game,

"That's my son, that's my son."

He ignored him 'til now

Johnny's body, brain is

pummeled, smashed at every game

At some point he may not be able to

walk, talk, see, hear

But to his father it doesn't matter

Johnny was always disposable

Final Thought

A Love Letter

I fed you organics
I gave you potions
Lotions sweet smelling

You got me up Swiss mountains
and let me hike all day
Unbelievable beauty

When we lived in the city
Exploring, wandering
We never took wheels

But now you are robbing me
At bottom of flight of stairs
I calculate, can I make it to the top

You say you have had your four score
I want another score
Do not take away my passion

I know there is an expiration date
Let me die without pain
        in my sleep
For all that we have been through

But until then
Let me go and do and be

MarlouNewkirk.com

www.ingramcontent.com/pod-product-compliance
Lightning Source LLC
Chambersburg PA
CBHW040743250626
47164CB00001BA/18